D0476884

IMAGINE THAT™
Licensed exclusively to Imagine That Publishing Ltd
Tide Mill Way, Woodbridge, Suffolk, IP12 1AP, UK
www.imaginethat.com

2 4 6 8 9 7 5 3 1
Manufactured in China

Illustrated by Doreen Marts
Written by Rose Williamson

ISBN 978-1-78700-900-4

A catalogue record for this book is available from the British Library

Look at me! Look at me!

by Rose Williamson

Cammy Chameleon lived in a tree and was very good at hiding. Cammy turned brown on a brown branch and green on a green leaf.

It made it very easy to
sneak up on yummy bugs!

But Cammy didn't want to hide. She thought she was a very beautiful chameleon indeed and she wanted all of the other animals to look at her.

She called out to the tree frogs,
'Look at me! Look at me!'

But the tree frogs could
not see a green chameleon
on a green leaf.

She called out to the lemurs,
'Look at me! Look at me!'

But the lemurs could not see a brown chameleon on a brown branch.

Cammy was very upset that no one could see her. She began to wonder what it would be like if she didn't always blend in …

Cammy climbed down from her tree and
concentrated very, very hard ...

And turned red!

'Look at me! Look at me!'
she called to the tree frogs.
'What a beautiful chameleon!' they said.

Cammy practised changing colour all day.
She was pink on a grey stone ...

She was black on yellow sand ...

She was purple on
an orange flower …

… and orange on
a purple flower.

'Look at me! Look at me!'
she called to the lemurs.
'What a beautiful
chameleon!' they said.

Cammy thought she was
the most beautiful chameleon
in the whole world.

Soon, she began to feel hungry
and went home to her tree.

Cammy climbed onto her brown branch and waited for a yummy bug. She waited and waited.

She watched the other chameleons catching bugs on their sticky tongues and her stomach rumbled. She was very hungry!

Then, Cammy saw a group of bugs nearby! But, before she could stick out her long tongue, they saw her beautiful colours and flew away!

‘What a beautiful chameleon!’
the laughing bugs called to her.

Suddenly, Cammy felt very silly.
A colourful chameleon couldn't hide
like a plain brown chameleon!

Cammy knew that to catch bugs,
she would need to blend in so she
concentrated very, very hard ...

and changed colour so that she
blended in with her surroundings!

Cammy had learnt that it is not good to show off and was happy being a regular chameleon again.

But sometimes, just every once in a while,
Cammy concentrates very, very hard ...